CALL OF FRIENDSHIP

~Unmasking the Hidden Culprit

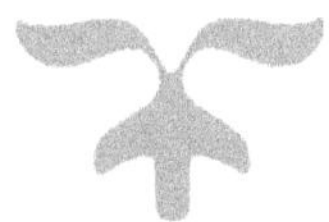

~UTKARSH KUMAR

including without limitation, indirect or consequential loss or damage arising out of use, inability to use, or about the reliability, accuracy or sufficiency of the information contained in this book.

Foreword

Preface

Acknowledgements

Prologue

1. A Visit to The Hospital

2. The First Step

3. Echoes Of the Past

4. Preparation For a New Journey

5. Old Connections, New Beginnings

6. New Bonds, New Challenges

7. The Real Search Begins

8. Formation Of New Relation

9. Love & Deception

10. The Confession

11. Beginning Of New Chapter

Author's Description

Foreword

In every heart lies a story of resilience, vengeance, and the quest for justice. This novella, "Call of Friendship," delves into the intricate dance between light and darkness, truth and deception, love and betrayal. It is a tale that not only captures the essence of human struggle but also the indomitable spirit that drives us to seek justice, no matter the cost.

The story of Trisha and Mayra begins in the innocent halls of an orphanage, where a bond of friendship forms out of shared pain and mutual support. As their lives take different paths, the story takes us on a journey through time, unravelling the mysteries of the past and the complexities of the present. Trisha's journey from a tormented child to a determined avenger is both heart-wrenching and inspiring, highlighting the impact of our experiences on our choices and actions.

At its core, this novella explores the themes of loyalty and betrayal, the blurred lines between right and wrong, and the relentless pursuit of truth. Trisha's quest to find Mayra's assailant, coupled with her own dark past, challenges readers to consider the lengths to which one can go to protect loved ones and achieve justice.

The characters in this story are a reflection of our own struggles and triumphs. Trisha, with her sharp mind and hardened heart, embodies the strength born from pain. Mayra, even in her silence, symbolizes hope and resilience. Satya, with his duality, reminds us of the masks people wear and the hidden truths they conceal.

As you read "Call Of Friendship," I invite you to immerse yourself in the world of these characters. Feel their pain, rejoice in their victories, and ponder the moral dilemmas they face. This is more than a story of revenge; it is a testament to the enduring human spirit and the power of friendship and love in the face of adversity.

I hope this novella leaves you with a sense of reflection and a deeper understanding of the complexities of human nature. May it inspire you to seek truth, fight for justice, and cherish the bonds that define us.

Thank you for embarking on this journey with Trisha and Mayra. Their story is now yours.

~Utkarsh Kumar

Preface

"Call Of Friendship" is a story that emerged from the depths of imagination, fueled by the desire to explore the complexities of human nature and the eternal struggle between good and evil. Within these pages, readers will embark on a journey through the intertwined lives of Trisha and Mayra, two souls bound together by fate and circumstance.

In crafting this narrative, I was inspired by the resilience of the human spirit and the relentless pursuit of justice in the face of adversity. Through the lens of our protagonists, we delve into themes of friendship, betrayal, redemption, and the quest for truth.

This novella is a testament to the power of storytelling to illuminate the darkest corners of our hearts and minds. It invites readers to contemplate the moral ambiguities of life, to empathize with characters who grapple with their own demons, and to ponder the choices that define their destinies.

As you turn the pages of "Call Of Friendship," I encourage you to immerse yourself fully in the world created within these words. Let yourself be drawn into the drama, the suspense, and the emotion that unfolds with each chapter. And as you journey alongside Trisha and Mayra, may you discover the enduring strength of the human spirit and the transformative power of love and friendship.

~Utkarsh Kumar

Acknowledgements

First and foremost, I would like to express my deepest gratitude to my family and friends for their unwavering support and encouragement throughout the process of writing this novella. Your belief in me has been a constant source of motivation.

To my mother, who has always been my biggest cheerleader, thank you for your love, patience, and for nurturing my passion for storytelling from a young age. Your guidance has been invaluable.

I owe a special thanks to my friend Amritesh Hreeshabh and Raj Nandini who offered their insights and feedback, and who were always there to listen to my ideas and provide constructive criticism. Your contributions have helped shape this story into what it is today.

Lastly, I want to thank my readers. Your enthusiasm and support mean the world to me. I hope this story resonates with you and that you enjoy reading it as much as I enjoyed writing it.

Thank you all for being a part of this journey with me.

Prologue

In the shadows of the world, where darkness lurks and secrets lie buried, there exists a realm of whispered truths and concealed betrayals. It is within this clandestine realm that our story begins, where the threads of fate weave a tangled web of destiny and despair.

In the heart of a bustling city, amidst the chaos and clamour of everyday life, stands a lone figure shrouded in mystery and intrigue. Trisha, a woman haunted by her past and driven by an insatiable thirst for justice, prowls the streets with determination etched into her very being. Her journey is a solitary one, fueled by the memories of a childhood scarred by pain and loss.

But Trisha is not alone in her quest. Beside her walks Mayra, a beacon of light in a world consumed by darkness. Together, they navigate the treacherous waters of deceit and deception, their bond forged in the fires of adversity. Yet even as they strive to uncover the truth, a shadow looms on the horizon, threatening to engulf them in its malevolent embrace.

As the story unfolds, secrets will be revealed, alliances will be tested, and the line between friend and foe will blur beyond recognition. For in this world of shadows and vengeance, nothing is as it seems, and trust is a commodity in short supply.

So it is that our tale begins, in the murky depths of the human soul, where the battle between light and dark rages on. Join us, dear reader, as we embark on a journey fraught with peril and possibility, where the only certainty is uncertainty, and the only truth is the one we seek to uncover.

~Utkarsh Kumar

CHAPTER-1: A VISIT TO THE HOSPITAL

Trisha's phone buzzed relentlessly, pulling her from the depths of a dreamless sleep. She groaned, rolling over and fumbling for the phone on her nightstand. The harsh light of the screen made her squint as she read the caller ID: it was a number from India. Her heart skipped a beat, a cold shiver running down her spine. Calls from home were rare, and they never brought good news. She hesitated for a moment before answering.

"Hello?" Her voice was thick with sleep, shaky.

"Is this Trisha?" The voice on the other end was stern, authoritative.

"Yes, who's calling?"

"This is Inspector Rathi from the Mumbai Police. I'm calling about your friend, Mayra. She's been attacked and is in critical condition at City Hospital."

Trisha sat up abruptly, the sleep fog clearing instantly from her mind. "What happened?" she demanded, her voice rising in panic.

"She was found unconscious with severe injuries. We're investigating it as an attempted murder. We need you to come to India as soon as possible."

Trisha felt her world tilt, her heart pounding wildly. "I'll be on the next flight," she said, her voice steadying with resolve.

The line went dead, leaving Trisha clutching the phone in a vice grip. She swung her legs over the side of the bed, her mind racing. Mayra, her best friend, her sister in everything but blood, was fighting for her life. The thought was unbearable, a sharp knife twisting in her heart.

She stood up, her movements mechanical as she began to pack a bag. The room around her felt surreal, the familiar surroundings of her apartment in stark contrast to the turmoil inside her. She grabbed clothes, toiletries, her passport, her hands shaking. Each item she packed seemed insignificant, trivial in the face of the news she had just received.

The flight was a blur. Trisha barely registered the journey, her mind consumed with worry and fear. She tried to piece together what could have happened, who could have wanted to hurt Mayra. Her thoughts kept circling back to the last time they had spoken, Mayra's voice cheerful and full of life. It seemed impossible that anything could have happened to her.

As the plane touched down in Mumbai, Trisha felt a wave of nausea. The city, with its chaotic energy and familiar smells, was both comforting and overwhelming. She navigated through the crowded airport, her eyes darting around, searching for a sign, a clue, anything.

She took a taxi straight to City Hospital, her hands clenched in her lap. The driver weaved through the traffic with practiced ease, the cacophony of horns and shouts barely registering in Trisha's mind. She stared out the window, watching the city flash by in a blur of colours and movement. Then suddenly the taxi stopped and the driver said, we have reached the City hospital.

A formidable presence stands before Trisha, casting a shadow over her already burdened heart. As it looms overhead, imposing and unyielding, its towering walls, a symphony of concrete and glass, seem to echo the weight of the world below in an echo of their imposing and unyielding presence. The sterile facade, lacking in warmth or comfort, serves as a strong reminder of the fragility of life inside.

As Trisha steps out of the taxi, the clamour of the bustling city fades into the background, replaced by the deafening thud of her own heartbeat. Each step towards the entrance is heavy with apprehension, her every movement a testament to the gravity of the situation at hand.

With trembling hands, Trisha pushes through the heavy doors of the hospital, the cool rush of air washing over her like a wave of uncertainty. The lobby stretches out before her—a maze of corridors and waiting rooms that seem to stretch into infinity.

Approaching the reception desk, Trisha is met with a sea of faces, seemed to mirror her own inner fears and uncertainties. Despite the receptionist's courteous smile, Trisha couldn't shake the tight knot of anxiety in her stomach as she grappled to articulate the depth of her emotions.

"I-I'm here to see Mayra," Trisha stammers, her voice barely above a whisper as she meets the receptionist's gaze.

The receptionist nods, her eyes soft with sympathy as she gestures towards the elevator. "Room 302," she says gently. "Take the third floor, turn left, and it'll be the third room on your right."

Trisha nods, her heart pounding in her chest as she makes her way towards the elevator. Each floor ticks by agonizingly slowly, each ding of the elevator a harsh reminder of the precious moments slipping away.

The antiseptic scent of the hospital assaulted Trisha's senses as she stepped through the sterile corridors after the opening of elevator's doors with a soft chime, her heart heavy with apprehension. Twenty years apart had done little to dull the bond she shared with Mayra, her childhood friend from the orphanage. Now, as she made her way to Mayra's bedside, Trisha's mind raced with worry, each step echoing the uncertainty of what lay ahead.

Room 302 waits at the end of the corridor, its door closed and forbidding. Trisha hesitates for a moment, her hand trembling as she reaches out to grasp the doorknob. With a deep breath, she pushes open the door, her heart in her throat as she steps inside. Her eyes fell upon her friend's pale, fragile form lying motionless on the hospital bed. Tubes and wires snaked around her, tethering her to the realm of the living. As Trisha saw this, a wave of emotions crashes over her and breath caught in her throat as she approached, her hand reaching out to grasp Mayra's cold, clammy fingers. Her fingers brushing against Mayra's hand, the warmth of her touch a balm to her wounded soul.

"Mayra," Trisha whispers, her voice barely audibles above the hum of the machines and choked on emotion. "It's me, Trisha. I'm here."

But Mayra remains unresponsive, lost in the depths of unconsciousness. Trisha's heart aches at the sight, a pang of guilt gnawing at her insides as she recalls the events that led to this moment. If only she had been there, if only she had known sooner, perhaps she could have prevented this tragedy from unfolding.

Suddenly, Mayra stirred at the continuous sound of her name, her eyelids fluttering open to reveal her eyes clouded with pain and confusion. Recognition dawned

slowly on her features as she struggled to focus on Trisha's face. Mayra's lips trembled, desperate to speak, but no words escaped. Trisha could see the frustration in her eyes, the unspoken words begging to be set free. It was a painful realization that their conversation would have to wait, as Mayra's body remained trapped in the realm of unconsciousness.

As Trisha nodded, tears welled up in her eyes. She couldn't speak past the lump in her throat. It was like the years melted away, leaving only the two of them, bound by a friendship forged in adversity.

Trisha settled into the chair beside Mayra's bed, the steady beep of the heart's monitors a constant reminder of the fragility of life, the weight of their shared history hung heavy in the air. Trisha knows that her journey is only just beginning. With each passing moment, she draws strength from the bond she shares with her friend, a bond that transcends time and space, a bond that will guide her through the darkness and into the light.

Trisha's thoughts drifted back to their days at the orphanage. She remembered the first time she had met Mayra, a spirited girl who had defended her against bullies. Trisha had been a quiet, withdrawn child, haunted by the trauma of her past. Mayra's kindness and courage had pulled her out of her shell, giving her the strength to face her fears.

She remembered the nights they had spent talking in whispers, sharing their hopes and dreams. Mayra had always wanted to make a difference, to help those who couldn't help themselves. It was no surprise that she had become a social activist, dedicating her life to fighting for justice.

Despite the silence, a silent vow took root in Trisha's heart, a promise to uncover the truth about Mayra's condition, no matter the cost. With a renewed sense of purpose, Trisha was determined to uncover the mystery of Mayra's illness and help her find renewed hope.

Leaning closer to Mayra, she whispers fiercely, "I promise you, Mayra, I will take revenge on those who did this to you."

The door creaked open behind her, and Trisha turned to see a nurse entering the room. The woman's face was kind, her eyes full of sympathy.

"Visiting hours are almost over," she said gently. "You can come back tomorrow."

Trisha nodded, reluctant to leave Mayra's side. She leaned down and kissed her friend's forehead. "I'll be back," she whispered. "I promise."

CHAPTER-2: THE FIRST STEP

Trisha steps out of the hospital room, the weight of her vow heavy on her shoulders. The sterile smell of disinfectant fills her nostrils as she makes her way back through the labyrinthine corridors of the hospital. Each step she takes feels like a small victory, a step closer to avenging Mayra.

The elevator doors close with a soft ding behind her, and Trisha punches the ground floor button with more force than necessary. She watches the numbers descend, her mind racing with thoughts of where to begin. The police station is the obvious first stop, but she knows from experience that official channels often lead to dead ends.

As she steps out into the bright sunlight, Trisha pulls her jacket tighter around her. The warmth of the day does little to thaw the chill that's settled deep in her bones. She needs answers, and she needs them now, so she went to the local police station to learn more about the incident and the person responsible for Mayra's condition. As Trisha stood at the threshold of the local police station, her eyes taking in every detail of the imposing building's grand exterior. The towering structure seemed to dwarf her, and as she hesitantly stepped inside, the heavy wooden doors creaked ominously. The air inside was thick with a mix of tension and suspicion, and the officers' eyes seemed to follow her every move, with their expressions unwelcoming and cold which added to the weight of the atmosphere, making Trisha feel even smaller in the vast, intimidating space.

She approaches the front desk, where a bored-looking officer barely glances up from his paperwork. Trisha says, trying to keep her voice steady, despite the rising tide of frustration within her. "I'm here to inquire about my friend, Mayra Gupta. I need to know if any progress has been made in her case."

The officer behind the desk sneer. "So, who are you to her?". He asked with a scoff "Another nosy person with a wild imagination, probably."

Trisha's frustration was palpable as she clenched her jaw, her nails digging into the soft flesh of her palms, leaving crescent-shaped imprints. Her eyes narrowed with determination as she fought to control her swirling emotions. "I'm her friend," she said through gritted teeth, her voice tinged with tension. "I will not allow myself a moment's rest until I untangle the enigma of what happened to her, and bring justice to light."

The officer sighs, his fingers tapping a rhythm on the desk. "You'll need to speak with Detective Collins. But he's busy right now. Come back later."

Trisha's frustration flares. "This can't wait. My friend was murdered, and I need to know what the police are doing about it."

The officer looks up, meeting her gaze for the first time. There's a flicker of something in his eyes—pity, perhaps—but it's quickly masked by a veneer of indifference. "Listen, ma'am, we've got procedures. If you want information, you'll have to wait."

Trisha's fists clench at her sides. "Fine," she snaps. "I'll wait."

She finds a seat in the corner of the waiting area, her mind a whirlwind of anger and determination. Memories of her past begin to surface, unbidden and unwelcome. She remembers the nights spent hiding from her father, the fear and helplessness that gripped her as he raged in his drunken stupor.

One particular night stands out. She was twelve, and her father had come home late, the stench of alcohol thick on his breath. He had found her in the kitchen, trying to clean up the mess he had left behind from the night before. His anger was swift and brutal, and for a moment, she thought she might not survive.

But something inside her snapped that night. She fought back, her small fists flying as she screamed for him to stop. And when he didn't, when his blows became more vicious, she grabbed the nearest object—a heavy, cast-iron skillet—and swung it with all her might.

The impact was sickening, and her father crumpled to the floor. The relief was immediate, but so was the fear. She knew what she had done, and she knew there would be consequences. The police came, and she was taken away, a twelve-year-old girl charged with manslaughter.

Juvenile detention was a harsh reality, but it was there that she met Malik. An older inmate with a quiet strength, Malik took her under his wing. He taught her how to defend herself, how to harness her anger and use it as a weapon. Under his guidance, she learned martial arts, discipline, and most importantly, survival.

The sound of her name pulls Trisha from her reverie. A stern-looking man in a rumpled suit stands before her, a clipboard in hand. "Trisha? I'm Detective Collins. Come with me."

She follows him through a maze of desks and filing cabinets, finally arriving at a small, cluttered office. Collins gestures for her to sit, then closes the door behind him. "I'm sorry for your loss," he begins, his tone businesslike. "We're doing everything we can to find out what happened to your friend."

Trisha leans forward, her eyes fixed on the detective. "I need to know if you've found any clues, any leads. I can't just sit back and do nothing."

Collins sighs, running a hand through his thinning hair. "I understand your frustration, but these things take time. We have a few leads, but nothing concretes yet."

Trisha's patience is wearing thin. "I don't have time, Detective. Mayra was my best friend, my only family. I have to find out who did this."

Collins studies her for a moment, then nods. "Alright. Here's what I can tell you. We believe Mayra's death is connected to a string of similar incidents. We're looking into possible suspects, but we need more evidence."

Trisha's mind races. A string of similar incidents? Could there be a pattern? "Can I see the case files?"

The detective hesitates, then shakes his head. "I'm sorry, but that's classified information. I can't share that with you."

Frustration bubbles up again, but Trisha forces it down. She needs a different approach. "Is there anything at all you can tell me? Anything that might help?"

Collins leans back in his chair, considering her request. "Off the record, there's a name that keeps coming up—Vikram. We don't know much about him, but he's on our radar. That's all I can give you."

Trisha nods, grateful for the small lead. It's not much, but it's a start. "Thank you, Detective."

As she leaves the station, Trisha's mind is already working on her next move. She knew she couldn't do this alone. She needs more information about this Vikram

She knows just the person who might be able to help—Malik. Her thoughts turned to Malik, an old mentor from her time in juvenile detention. He had taught her how to defend herself, how to survive. If anyone could help her now, it was him. He has connections in the criminal underworld that could prove invaluable.

She pulls out her phone and dials Malik's number, hoping he hasn't changed it. After a few rings, a familiar voice answer. "Trisha, it's been a while."

"Malik, I need your help," she says, wasting no time on pleasantries. "It's about Mayra. She's been murdered, and I need to find out who did it."

There's a pause on the other end, then Malik's voice comes through, steady and reassuring. "Come to the usual place. We'll talk."

Trisha ends the call, a sense of purpose filling her. With Malik's help, she'll track down this Vikram and anyone else involved.

And when she does, they will pay for what they've done to Mayra.

CHAPTER-3: ECHOES OF THE PAST

Trisha sits in a dingy corner of the café, her fingers wrapped around a lukewarm cup of coffee. The usual place, as Malik had called it, is a modest eatery hidden in the city's underbelly, where the lines between right and wrong often blur. She has a few minutes before Malik arrives, and in that quiet moment, her mind drifts back to the days when life was simpler, when she and Mayra first met and forged an unbreakable bond.

The orphanage stood at the edge of the city, a sprawling old building with ivy-covered walls and creaky wooden floors. It was here, amidst the chaos of children and the stern supervision of caretakers, that Trisha's and Mayra's paths first crossed.

Trisha was ten, with wild curls that framed her face and eyes that seemed too wise for her age. She often kept to herself, her small frame hunched in the corner of the room, watching the world with a guarded expression. Her clothes were always a size too big, hand-me-downs that hung loosely on her thin frame. The other children steered clear of her, sensing the quiet storm that brewed within her.

Mayra, on the other hand, was a beacon of light in the otherwise dreary orphanage. At eleven, she had a vibrant smile that could light up the darkest room and an infectious laugh that echoed through the hallways. Her hair, a cascade of dark waves, was always neatly tied back with a bright ribbon. She had a knack for finding joy in the smallest things—a butterfly flitting past the window, the taste of freshly baked cookies, the warmth of a summer's day.

Their friendship began on a rainy afternoon. Trisha was sitting by the window, her nose buried in a tattered book, when a group of older boys began teasing her. They snatched the book from her hands, tossing it back and forth, their taunts growing louder. Trisha's face flushed with anger and humiliation, but she didn't cry. She never cried.

It was then that Mayra stepped in. Without hesitation, she marched up to the boys, her hands on her hips and fire in her eyes. "Leave her alone!" she demanded, her voice steady and commanding.

The boys hesitated, momentarily taken aback by Mayra's fierce demeanor. But when she didn't back down, they reluctantly handed the book back to Trisha and slunk away, muttering under their breath.

"Are you okay?" Mayra asked, turning to Trisha with concern in her eyes.

Trisha nodded, clutching the book to her chest. "Thank you," she murmured, her voice barely audible. "This book was given to me by my mother before she... before she left. It's all I have of her."

Mayra's expression softened, a look of understanding passing between them. "I'm Mayra. Do you want to be friends?"

It was such a simple question, yet it held so much weight. Trisha looked at Mayra, really looked at her, and saw the kindness and strength in her eyes. "I'm Trisha," she replied, a small smile tugging at the corners of her lips. "And yes, I'd like that."

From that moment on, they were inseparable. They spent their days exploring the orphanage grounds, their imaginations transforming the old building into a magical kingdom where they were the queens. They shared secrets, dreams, and fears, their bond growing stronger with each passing day.

Trisha's mind drifts back to one particular memory, a warm summer evening when the air was filled with the scent of blooming flowers. They had sneaked out to the orphanage's rooftop, a secret hideaway they had discovered. Lying on their backs, they gazed up at the stars, their hands clasped together.

"Do you ever wonder what it would be like to have a real family?" Mayra asked, her voice soft and wistful.

Trisha turned her head to look at her friend, the starlight reflecting in her eyes. "Sometimes. But as long as I have you, I'm okay."

Mayra squeezed her hand. "We'll always have each other, no matter what."

It was a promise, a vow that they both held close to their hearts. And even as the years passed and they grew older, that promise remained unbroken.

CHAPTER-4: PREPARATION FOR A NEW JOURNEY

Trisha is pulled back to the present as the bell above the café door jingles. Malik steps in, his presence commanding attention even in the dimly lit room. He scans the café, his eyes landing on Trisha. With a nod, he makes his way over to her table.

"Trisha," he greets, his voice a low rumble. He slides into the seat across from her, his eyes sharp and focused. "It's been too long."

"Malik, I need your help." Trisha replies, her voice steady. "Mayra's been attacked, and I need to find out who did it."

Malik leans back in his chair, studying her for a moment. "I heard about Mayra. I'm sorry."

Trisha nods, her eyes hardening with resolve. "I need to find out who did this. The police mentioned a name—Vikram. Do you know anything about him?"

Malik's expression darkens. "Vikram is dangerous. He's connected to some very powerful people. But I have some contacts who might be able to help."

Trisha leans forward, her hands gripping the edge of the table. "Whatever it takes, Malik. I need to know who did this with Mayra."

Malik nods slowly. "Alright. There's someone you should meet. My Student, Satya. He's been keeping an eye on the criminal activities in this area. He might have some information for you."

Trisha feels a spark of hope. "Where can I find him?"

"I'll arrange a meeting," Malik says, pulling out his phone. "In the meantime, stay safe. You're walking into dangerous territory."

Trisha's eyes flash with determination. "I can handle it. For Mayra, I'll do whatever it takes."

As Malik makes the call, Trisha's thoughts drift back to the past once more. The memories of her and Mayra's time at the orphanage, the laughter, the tears, the unbreakable bond they shared—these are the things that fuel her determination. Mayra was more than a friend;

she was her family, her anchor in a world of chaos. And now, she would do whatever it took to honor that bond and seek justice for her fallen friend.

she felt a renewed sense of purpose. She wasn't alone in this fight. With Malik and Satya's help, she would uncover the truth and make sure that Mayra's attacker paid for what they had done.

The journey ahead was fraught with danger, but Trisha was ready. She would not rest until justice was served, until the person responsible for Mayra's suffering was brought to justice.

The memory of Mayra's smile, her laughter, and her unwavering strength filled Trisha's mind, fueling her determination. She would not let her friend down. No matter what it took, she would find the culprit and make them pay.

And with that promise burning in her heart, Trisha set out

CHAPTER-5: OLD CONNECTION, NEW BEGINNINGS

Malik's call doesn't take long. Within minutes, he has arranged a meeting with Satya. Trisha's mind races with thoughts of what this encounter will bring. Malik has always been a figure of strength and guidance in her life, and if Satya is anything like his father, she knows she will be in capable hands. Still, a flicker of uncertainty gnaws at her—she's venturing into the unknown, trusting people with her heart and her mission.

The café door swings open again, and Malik motions for Trisha to follow him. They walk in silence, the streets buzzing with the activity of everyday life. Trisha's senses are on high alert, every noise and movement magnified by the urgency of her quest. They arrive at a nondescript building, the kind that blends into the background of the bustling city. Malik leads her inside, through a dimly lit hallway, and up a flight of narrow stairs.

At the top, they reach a door marked with a single letter: S. Malik knocks, a coded rhythm that seems to speak volumes. The door opens, revealing a tall, lean man with sharp features and an intense gaze. Satya.

"Trisha, this is my student, Satya," Malik says, placing a hand on Satya's shoulder. "Satya, this is Trisha. She needs our help."

Satya's eyes meet Trisha's, and she feels a jolt of something she can't quite identify. Respect? Curiosity? Perhaps a bit of both. "I've heard a lot about you," Satya says, his voice calm and measured. "Come in."

The room they step into is a stark contrast to the hallway—a well-organized space filled with monitors, maps, and files. It's clear that Satya runs a tight operation, his attention to detail evident in every aspect of his surroundings.

"Please, sit," Satya gestures to a pair of chairs near a cluttered desk. Trisha and Malik take their seats, while Satya remains standing, his presence commanding the room. "I understand you're looking for someone named Vikram."

Trisha nods. "He's connected to Mayra's murder. I need to find him."

Satya's expression hardens. "Vikram is dangerous. He's involved in a lot of illegal activities—trafficking, extortion, you name it. Tracking him won't be easy, but I have some leads."

Malik chimes in, his voice steady. "Satya has contacts in the underworld. If anyone can find Vikram, it's him."

Trisha feels a surge of hope. "Thank you, both of you. I can't do this alone."

Satya gives a curt nod. "We'll start by gathering more information. I have a few people I can reach out to, but it will take some time. In the meantime, you need to stay under the radar. Vikram has eyes everywhere."

The days that follow are a blur of strategy sessions, covert meetings, and information gathering. Trisha spends hours with Satya, poring over maps and documents, piecing together the puzzle that is Vikram's network. She is impressed by Satya's intelligence and dedication, his sharp mind constantly at work. Despite the gravity of their mission, there are moments of levity—shared stories, quiet laughter—that begin to forge a bond between them.

One evening, as they sit in Satya's office, Trisha finds herself opening up about her past, about the book her mother gave her, and the night she met Mayra. Satya listens intently, his eyes never leaving hers.

"You've been through a lot," he says softly. "But it's made you stronger."

Trisha nods, feeling a lump form in her throat. "Mayra was my anchor. Losing her... it's like losing a part of myself."

Satya reaches out, placing a reassuring hand on hers. "We'll find justice for her. I promise."

In that moment, something shifts between them. A connection, deeper than before, begins to take root. Trisha feels a flicker of something she hasn't felt in a long time—hope.

The breakthrough comes late one night. Satya bursts into the room where Trisha is staying, a triumphant look on his face. "We found him," he announces. "Vikram is hiding out in an old warehouse on the outskirts of the city. We need to move quickly."

Trisha's heart pounds in her chest. This is it—the moment she's been waiting for. "Let's go," she says, her voice filled with determination.

As they prepare to leave, Malik pulls Trisha aside. "Be careful," he warns. "Vikram is dangerous. Trust Satya—he'll keep you safe."

Trisha nods, her resolve unwavering. "I will. Thank you, Malik. For everything."

With that, they set out, the city lights blurring into streaks as they race towards their destination. Satya drives with a focused intensity, his eyes fixed on the road ahead. Trisha sits beside him, her mind a whirlwind of thoughts and emotions.

"Are you ready for this?" Satya asks, glancing at her.

Trisha meets his gaze, her eyes burning with resolve. "I've been ready my whole life."

They arrive at the warehouse, the air thick with tension. Satya leads the way, his movements swift and silent. Trisha follows close behind, her senses heightened. The building looms before them, a dark silhouette against the night sky.

Satya signals for Trisha to wait, then slips inside, his figure blending into the shadows. Moments later, he returns, a grim look on his face. "He's here," he whispers. "Stay close."

They move through the warehouse, the air heavy with the scent of dust and decay. Trisha's heart races as they navigate the maze of crates and machinery, each step bringing them closer to their target.

Finally, they reach a large, open space. Vikram stands at the center, flanked by his men. The moment he sees Trisha and Satya, a malicious smile

spreads across his face.

"Well, well," Vikram sneers. "What do we have here? A little reunion?"

Trisha steps forward, her eyes locked on Vikram. "This ends now," she says, her voice steady.

Vikram laughs, a harsh, grating sound. "You think you can stop me? You're just a girl."

Trisha's eyes narrow, her anger fueling her strength. "I'm more than that. I'm justice."

With a nod from Satya, the fight begins. Chaos erupts as Trisha and Satya take on Vikram's men, their movements fluid and precise. Trisha's training kicks in, each punch and kick a testament to the lessons she learned from Malik. Satya is a force of nature, his strength and agility unmatched.

In the midst of the battle, Trisha finds herself face-to-face with Vikram. The look in his eyes is one of pure malice, but she doesn't falter. She channels all her pain, all her loss, into her strikes, each one bringing her closer to justice for Mayra.

Finally, with one last, powerful blow, Vikram falls to the ground, unconscious. Trisha stands over him, her chest heaving with exertion. It's over. The man who took Mayra's life is defeated.

As the police arrive to take Vikram into custody, Trisha feels a sense of closure wash over her. She turns to Satya, a grateful smile on her face. "We did it," she says softly.

Satya nods, his eyes filled with admiration. "You did it, Trisha. You found justice for Mayra."

In that moment, Trisha realizes that she has found more than just justice—she has found a new family, a new beginning. And as she stands with Satya by her side, she knows that together, they can face whatever the future holds.

CHAPTER-6: NEW BONDS, NEW CHALLENGES

The days following Vikram's capture are a whirlwind of police reports and media attention. Trisha's story becomes a sensation, and she finds herself thrust into the spotlight. Through it all, Satya remains by her side, his quiet strength a constant source of support.

As the initial chaos begins to subside, Trisha and Satya find moments of peace amidst the storm. They spend time together, their bond growing stronger with each passing day. Satya's sharp wit and unwavering loyalty become a balm for Trisha's wounded heart.

One evening, as they sit on the rooftop of Satya's apartment, watching the sun set over the city, Trisha feels a deep sense of contentment. It's a feeling she hasn't experienced in a long time.

"Thank you," she says softly, breaking the comfortable silence.

Satya looks at her, a question in his eyes. "For what?"

"For everything," Trisha replies. "For helping me find justice for Mayra. For being there when I needed someone."

Satya reaches out, taking her hand in his. "You don't need to thank me. I'm just glad I could help."

Trisha smiles, her heart swelling with gratitude. "I don't know what I would have done without you."

Satya's eyes soften, and he leans in, pressing a gentle kiss to her forehead. "You would have found a way. You're stronger than you realize."

In that moment, Trisha knows that she has found something special in Satya—someone who understands her pain, who shares her drive for justice, and who is willing to stand by her no matter what.

Several weeks later, Trisha decided to revisit the detective who initially pointed them towards Vikram. Something about the case continues to nag at Trisha, a feeling she can't shake. They arrive at the detective's house just as the sun begins to set, casting long shadows over the quiet street.

As Trisha approaches the gate, she saw a police officer talking to Satya in hushed tone. The conversation is serious, the tension palpable. Trisha stops, and hide behind a nearby bush, straining to hear the conversation.

"...how we trapped Vikram, an innocent guy, by telling her a wrong story," Satya says, their voice low and gravelly.

Trisha's heart skips a beat. She exchanges a glance, her eyes wide with shock. Vikram was innocent? The implications of this revelation are staggering.

The police officer responds, his tone cold and calculated. "It was necessary. I needed a scapegoat to close the case quickly. No one will question it now."

Trisha feels a surge of anger and disbelief. She deceived. All efforts, quest for justice—it was based on a lie. She steps forward, her fists clenched, ready to confront them, but a sudden thought stops her to do so.

"Not here," she whispers. "I need to be smart about this."

She quietly retreats, making her way back to car. Once inside, she lets out a frustrated sigh, her mind racing with thoughts of betrayal and injustice.

"I need to expose them," Trisha says, her voice filled with determination. "I need to clear Vikram's name and find out who really killed Mayra."

CHAPTER-7: THE REAL SEARCH BEGINS

She came back to her flat and her thoughts drift back to the past, to the memories of her bad experiences

A young Trisha sits alone in a dimly lit room at the orphanage, hugging a worn-out book to her chest. The sounds of other children playing outside are distant, muted by the thick walls. This book, given to her by her mother before she passed away, is her most prized possession.

Trisha's father used to be a different man before alcohol consumed him. She remembers the early days when her mother was alive— moments filled with laughter and love. But those memories are overshadowed by the nights of terror that followed her mother's death.

One night, her father stumbles into the room, reeking of alcohol. His eyes are bloodshot, filled with a rage that she's all too familiar with. He starts yelling at her, calling her names, blaming her for everything wrong in his life.

In a fit of drunken honesty, he reveals the truth she had always feared. "I killed her! Your mother is dead because of me!"

The words pierce through Trisha like a knife. A surge of rage and fear fuels her actions. She grabs the knife from under her pillow—a knife she kept for protection—and plunges it into his chest, over and over until he stops moving.

The days that follow are filled with careful planning and discreet investigations. Trisha and Satya dig deeper into the case, uncovering discrepancies and gathering evidence to expose the corrupt police officer and his accomplice. Their bond grows stronger through the shared mission, each step bringing them closer to the truth.

Suddenly Malik called Trisha and Satya, informed them about Vikram's innocence from this case

On that evening, as they sit in Satya's office, surrounded by documents and notes, Trisha feels a renewed sense of purpose. They are closer than ever to uncovering the real culprit behind Mayra's murder.

"I can't believe we were so close to being misled," Trisha says, her voice tinged with frustration. "But now we have a chance to make things right."

Satya reaches out, taking her hand in his. "We will. Together."

In that moment, Trisha realizes that she has not only found a partner in her quest for justice but also someone who shares her unwavering determination and strength. Together, they are unstoppable.

With the truth about Vikram's innocence revealed, Trisha and Satya launch a renewed investigation to find Mayra's real murderer. The days blur into weeks, then months, as they dig deeper into the labyrinth of corruption and deceit that obscures the truth. They find themselves entangled in a complex web of leads, false trails, and hidden motives.

During this time, Trisha and Satya grow closer. The intensity of their mission forges a deep bond between them. They begin living together to streamline their efforts, sharing both the burdens of the investigation and moments of solace in each other's company. Slowly, their partnership evolves into something more profound.

CHAPTER-8: FORMATION OF NEW RELATION

One evening, they decide to take a break from their intense work. The air is cool and crisp as they walk to a nearby ice cream parlor. Satya insists on treating Trisha to her favorite flavor, and they settle on a bench outside, savoring their cones.

Trisha laughs as she tells Satya a story from her childhood, her eyes sparkling with warmth and nostalgia. Satya watches her, captivated by her vivacity and strength. Suddenly, Trisha frowns, trying to understand Satya's amused expression.

"What?" she asks, puzzled.

Satya chuckles softly, pointing at her. "You've got ice cream on your lips."

Trisha swipes at her mouth, missing the spot entirely. "Did I get it?"

Satya shakes his head, still smiling. "Here, let me help."

He leans in, his hand gently cupping her chin as he uses his thumb to wipe away the errant ice cream. His touch lingers, and their eyes lock. Trisha's breath catches in her throat as the world seems to pause around them.

In a moment of unspoken understanding, Satya leans closer, and their lips meet in a tender kiss. The kiss deepens, a mix of passion and unspoken promises. When they finally pull apart, Trisha's heart is pounding, and she can see the same intensity mirrored in Satya's eyes.

Back at their apartment, the atmosphere is charged with newfound intimacy. They talk late into the night, sharing their hopes and fears, their dreams and regrets. The connection between them grows stronger, fueled by both their shared mission and the deepening affection they feel for one another.

One night, as they lie side by side on the couch, Trisha looks over at Satya, her expression serious. "Thank you for being here with me, for supporting me through all of this," she says softly.

Satya turns to her, his gaze tender. "I wouldn't be anywhere else. We make a good team."

Trisha smiles, a warmth spreading through her. "We do."

Their lips meet again, and this time, there's no hesitation. They move together in perfect harmony, their kisses growing more fervent. Satya's hands slide under Trisha's shirt, his touch sending shivers down her spine. She responds by straddling him, her fingers threading through his hair as their kisses grow deeper and more urgent.

Trisha feels a rush of desire, an overwhelming need to be closer to Satya. She pulls back briefly, looking into his eyes, seeing the same desire reflected there. Without a word, she pulls off her shirt, and Satya follows suit, discarding his own shirt quickly.

Their hands explore each other's bodies, every touch igniting a fire within. Trisha leans down, her lips trailing along Satya's neck and chest, tasting his skin. Satya's hands roam over her back, pulling her closer. The room is filled with the sounds of their heavy breathing and the soft rustle of clothes being discarded.

As they continue to undress each other, their movements become more urgent, more desperate. Trisha kisses a trail down Satya's torso, her lips and tongue exploring every inch of him. Satya groans, his hands tangling in her hair, guiding her movements. When Trisha looks up, their eyes lock again, and the intensity of their connection is undeniable.

Satya flips them over, his body hovering over hers, his eyes dark with desire. He leans down, capturing her lips in a searing kiss as his hands continue to explore her body. Trisha arches into his touch, her own hands roaming over his muscular frame.

Their kisses grow hungrier, more demanding, as they lose themselves in each other. Satya's mouth moves to Trisha's neck, trailing kisses and gentle bites along her collarbone and down to her breasts. Trisha moans softly, her hands gripping his shoulders as she surrenders to the sensations coursing through her.

Satya takes his time, savoring every moment, every touch. He moves lower, his lips and tongue exploring her body with a tenderness that contrasts with the intensity of their desire. Trisha's breath hitches as Satya's mouth finds her most sensitive spots, his tongue flicking and teasing until she can barely stand it.

"Satya," she whispers, her voice trembling with need.

He looks up at her, his eyes dark with passion. "Trisha," he murmurs, his voice a low growl. "I need you."

Their eyes lock once more, and in that moment, everything else fades away. Satya moves back up to capture her lips in another deep, passionate kiss. Their bodies move together in perfect harmony, each touch, each kiss, bringing them closer to the edge.

Satya's hands tighten on Trisha's hips, guiding her movements with an urgency that matches their rising desire. Trisha reaches back, her fingers wrapping around his wrist, pulling him even closer. She feels his hardness throbbing against her, and she reaches down, guiding him back inside her with a determined motion. The sensation sends a shiver of pleasure through her, eliciting a deep moan from both of them.

"Yes, Satya," she breathes, her voice a mixture of command and plea. "Just like that."

Satya responds with a powerful thrust, filling her completely. Their rhythm becomes frenzied, each movement driving them closer to the brink. Trisha's body tenses, her cries growing louder with each thrust. She feels the heat building within her, an unstoppable wave of pleasure threatening to consume her.

"Faster," she urges, her voice breaking with intensity. "More... more."

Satya's pace quickens, his thrusts becoming more forceful, more precise. The sound of their bodies meeting fills the room, a symphony of their passion. Trisha's breath hitches, her entire body trembling as she feels the climax approaching, closer with each powerful movement.

As her climax overtakes her, Trisha's cries reach a fever pitch, her body quaking with the force of her release. Satya continues to drive into her, the sensation of her tightening around him pushing him over the edge. With a final, deep thrust, he feels his own release surging through him, spilling into her with a groan of pure satisfaction.

They collapse together, their bodies spent but still entwined. The aftermath is filled with the soft sounds of their heavy breathing, their hearts beating in unison. Trisha turns her head, meeting Satya's eyes with a look of deep contentment and love.

"I love you," she whispers, her voice soft and full of emotion.

Satya leans down, pressing a tender kiss to her lips. "I love you too, Trisha. Always."

CHAPTER-9: LOVE & DECEPTION

Trisha lies beside Satya, his steady breaths lulling her into a sense of security. But beneath the facade of intimacy, a dark determination fester within her. With trembling hands, she reaches for the knife hidden beneath the pillow, her heart pounding in her chest.

As Satya's arm wraps around her, pulling her closer, Trisha's grip tightens on the knife. With a swift, practiced motion, she plunges it into his chest, the shock of the betrayal registering on his face before his eyes slide shut, forever.

In the bathroom, Trisha stares at her reflection in the mirror, the blood of her lover staining her hands and face. But instead of horror, a twisted grin stretches across her lips. She watches as the blood drips down her chin, mingling with the tears of laughter that stream down her cheeks.

As she wipes away the blood, memories of her past flood her mind, each one a testament to her darkness. She sees herself as a child, standing over her father's lifeless body, the knife still clutched in her hand. The rage that consumed her that night, the satisfaction of seeing him pay for his sins—all of it washes over her in a wave of twisted euphoria.

Trisha finishes cleaning herself up. She takes a deep breath, steadying her nerves. She knows she has to act quickly. The police will soon arrive, and she needs to play her part perfectly.

As she steps out of the washroom, she hears the faint sound of sirens in the distance. She grabs her phone and calls Malik, her voice shaking with feigned panic. "Malik, Satya is dead. Someone killed him. I need your help."

Malik's response is immediate. "Stay where you are. I'll be there soon."

When Malik arrives, he finds Trisha sitting on the floor, tears streaming down her face. She plays the role of the devastated girlfriend perfectly, and Malik buys it completely. He pulls her into a comforting embrace, promising to help her through this.

"What happened?" Malik asks, his voice filled with concern.

Trisha looks up at him, her eyes red and swollen. "I don't know. We were just sitting here, and someone broke in. They attacked Satya and left. I couldn't do anything."

Malik nods, his face grim. "We'll find out who did this. I promise."

But as they sit together, Trisha's mind is already racing ahead, planning her next move as she has a doubt that one more who is still out there, and she won't rest until she doesn't clear her doubt. The stakes are higher than ever, and Trisha is prepared to do whatever it takes to see justice served.

CHAPTER-10:

THE

CONFESSION

Trisha sits in the hospital room, the steady beeping of machines providing a rhythmic backdrop to her racing thoughts. She watches Mayra, her best friend, lying in the bed, still and fragile. The sight tugs at her heart, a painful reminder of why she has done everything.

With a deep breath, Trisha leans forward, gently taking Mayra's hand in hers. "Mayra," she whispers, her voice trembling. "I did it. I killed Satya."

As she speaks, Trisha's mind drifts back to the moment she uncovered the truth. She had gone to the police station to thank the detective who had helped her so much in her quest for justice. She stood outside his office, preparing to knock, when she overheard a conversation that made her blood run cold.

Trisha stood frozen, just outside the detective's office, the voices inside muffled but clear enough to understand. The detective was speaking to someone—someone with a familiar voice.

"We've got her right where we want her," the detective said, his tone dripping with satisfaction. "Trisha won't know what hit her. Vikram was the perfect scapegoat."

"And Satya?" the other voice, low and menacing, replied.

"He's been keeping her busy. She thinks he's helping her, but he's just another pawn in the game."

Trisha felt her heart stop. Satya—her Satya—was part of the conspiracy. The realization hit her like a punch to the gut. She had to act quickly, to set things right.

Trisha's mind raced as she left the police station, her heart pounding with a mix of fear and determination. She knew she needed to find out why Satya was involved in this and what his true motives were. She began digging into his past, using every resource at her disposal.

It didn't take long for her to uncover the truth. Satya was running an illegal business, one that was deeply harmful to the environment. He was involved in illegal logging and mining operations, destroying forests and poisoning water supplies. Mayra, as a dedicated social activist, had been investigating his activities and had filed a case against him.

Trisha's heart ached as she pieced together the story. Satya had targeted Mayra because she was a threat to his operations. He had tried to silence her, and when that failed, he had conspired with the detective to frame Vikram and mislead Trisha.

Trisha's grip on Mayra's hand tightens as she continues. "I couldn't believe it at first. But then, I knew I had to trap Satya, to make him pay for what he did to you."

She looks at Mayra, her eyes filling with tears. "I pretended to love him. I let him believe that we were building something real. And then, when the moment was right, I killed him."

Trisha's voice breaks as she recalls the night she killed Satya. The intimate moment, the knife in her hand, the look of betrayal on his face. "I did it for you, Mayra. I did it because I couldn't let him get away with what he did."

She takes a deep breath, trying to steady her emotions. "After I killed him, I went to the bathroom to clean the blood off my face. I looked in the mirror, and I saw the same rage in my eyes that I had when I killed my father."

Trisha's mind flashes back to that night, the memory of her father's confession, the knife in her hand, the fury that drove her to kill him. She had vowed never to become that person again, but here she was, covered in blood, having killed once more.

She looks down at Mayra, willing her to wake up, to respond, to give her some sign that she understands

Just as Trisha is about to leave, she feels a faint squeeze on her hand. She turns back to Mayra and sees a tear rolling down her friend's cheek. Mayra's eyes flutter open, and she looks at Trisha with a mix of pain and gratitude. Her lips move slightly, and Trisha leans in to hear her.

"T-Two..." Mayra whispers, her voice barely audible. "Two people..."

Trisha's eyes widen in realization. Mayra's gesture and words indicate that there were two people involved in the attempt on her life. A surge of hope and determination fills Trisha's heart. Mayra's awakening and her clue about the second person renew Trisha's resolve to uncover the whole truth and bring everyone responsible to justice.

CHAPTER-11: BEGINNING OF NEW CHAPTER

Trisha knows that she cannot do this alone. She needs Malik's help, and she needs to be honest with him. She stands, gently placing Mayra's hand back on the bed, and leaves the room with a new sense of purpose.

She finds Malik waiting in the hallway, his expression a mix of concern and curiosity. "Trisha, are you okay?" he asks, his voice gentle.

Trisha takes a deep breath. "I need to talk to you, Malik. There's something you need to know."

Later that evening, Trisha and Malik sit in a small café, the hum of conversations around them barely registering as Trisha gathers her thoughts. Malik watches her, sensing the weight of what she is about to reveal.

"Malik, there's something I need to tell you," Trisha begins, her voice barely above a whisper.

She takes a deep breath, steeling herself. "I… I killed Satya."

Malik's eyes widen in shock. "What? But why? You loved him, Trisha."

Tears well up in Trisha's eyes as she nods. "I did. Or at least, I thought I did. But I found out that he was one of the people responsible for Mayra's condition. He was involved in an illegal business that Mayra was trying to expose. When she became a threat, he tried to have her killed."

Malik leans back, stunned. "Satya… I can't believe it."

"I couldn't either, at first," Trisha continues, her voice trembling. "But the evidence was clear. Satya was running illegal logging and mining operations. He was destroying forests, poisoning water supplies, and Mayra was onto him. She had filed a case against him, and he tried to silence her."

Malik shakes his head, trying to process the information. "So, you killed him?"

Trisha nods, a tear slipping down her cheek. "I had to. After I found out the truth, I pretended to still love him. I let him believe we were building something real. And then, when the moment was right, I killed him. I couldn't let him get away with what he did to Mayra."

Malik reaches across the table, taking Trisha's hand in his. "You did what you had to do, Trisha. But we still need to find the second person involved. We need to finish what Mayra started."

Trisha squeezes his hand, grateful for his understanding. "We will, Malik. We'll find them, and we'll make sure they pay for what they did."

To Be Continued in the 2nd Part

Author's Description

I am a high school student with a deep passion for storytelling, and "Call of Friendship" is my very first book. Writing has always been my escape, my way of exploring new worlds and expressing my imagination. "Call Of friendship" is the culmination of years of dreaming and imagining. Despite my youth, I pour my heart and soul into every word, crafting characters and worlds that I hope will captivate readers and transport them to new realms of adventure and intrigue. With this debut novella, I hope you liked it!